OFF *to the* FAIR

Christopher Wormell

A Tom Maschler Book

Jonathan Cape · London

"Why, look at this," said Mr Bear. "There's a fair in town."
"Oh, we must go!" said Mrs Elephant.
"It'll be fun!" said Mrs Walrus.

"We'll go straight there," said Mr Bear.

So that's just what they did. Off they went and by and by they reached the town and followed the road to the fair.

B ut on the way they passed the shops.
"What lovely hats!" said Mrs Elephant.
"And swimsuits too!" said Mrs Walrus.

And in they went to have a look.
"Oh, do be quick," said Mr Bear.
"We'll miss the fun of the fair."

All the lovely hats were a bit too small for Mrs Elephant.
"Must you try *every* one?" complained Mr Bear.
And all the swimsuits were a bit too tight for a walrus.

"Oh, do come on!" said Mr Bear. "We'll be late for the fair, and I'm told they've a hall of mirrors there."

So off they went.

B ut on the way they passed the café.
"Shopping is such hot work, I must have an ice cream,"
declared Mrs Elephant.

"Me too!" agreed Mrs Walrus.
"Just a quick one perhaps," said Mr Bear.

But the ice creams were so tiny...

they had twenty-four each!

And made rather a mess. The waiter got cross.

Mr Bear got impatient. "Do let's get on to the fair. I'm sure they have candyfloss there."

So off they went.

B ut on the way they passed the cinema.
"Oh look," cried Mrs Elephant. "There's a film about a
small elephant with very large ears."

"But what about the fair?" said Mr Bear.
"We have all day to go there," said Mrs Walrus.

So in they went.

B ut all they saw at the cinema was the shadow of a large
elephant with very small ears.
"Well that was boring," grumbled Mr Bear when they came out.

"Now please can we go the fair? They may have a ghost train there."

So off they went.

But on the way they passed the swimming pool.
"Who's for a swim?" asked Mrs Elephant. "Just the thing after that
stuffy old cinema."

"And that sticky ice cream!" agreed Mrs Walrus.
And even Mr Bear thought it might be fun.

So – one, two, three – they all jumped in...

splash!

But when they jumped in most of the water jumped out!
And there wasn't much left for a swim.

"That was a washout," grumbled Mr Bear. "Now do let's hurry to the fair. I bet they have a helter-skelter there."

So off they went.

But on the way they passed a concert hall.
"I love a good concert," declared Mrs Elephant.
"Especially after a swim," added Mrs Walrus.

The concert was lovely...until Mrs Elephant began tapping her foot to the rhythm.

Everything shook as if there was an earthquake. The animals had
to leave.
"Perhaps *now* we can go to the fair?" said the exasperated Mr Bear.
"I've heard they have an organ there!"

So off they went.

But when they got there the gates were locked and everyone
had gone home to bed.
"Oh dear," said Mrs Elephant.
"What a shame," said Mrs Walrus.

"I *told* you to hurry," said Mr Bear angrily.
"Not to worry, Mr Bear," said Mrs Elephant. "We'll wait until it opens in the morning."

So that's what they did, they slept right there. And when the gates opened next morning they were first in the queue and they went straight in.

And there *was* a hall of mirrors and candyfloss and a ghost train and a helter-skelter. They all rode on the lovely merry-go-round but Mr Bear had four extra turns.

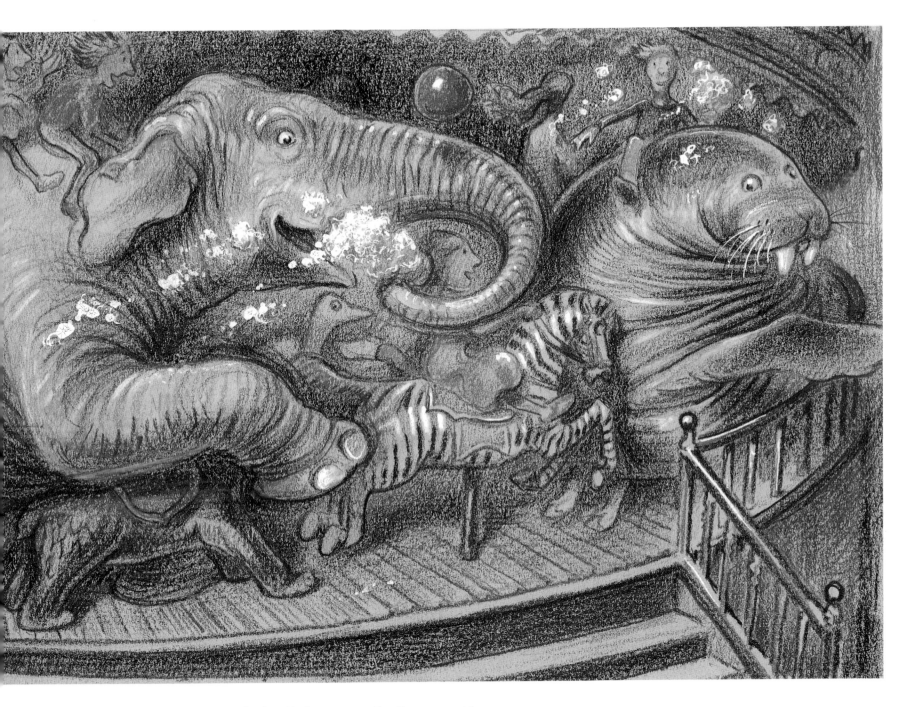

"This is the life," he said dreamily.

"I might come again tomorrow."

For Mary

First published 2001
1 3 5 7 9 10 8 6 4 2
© Christopher Wormell 2001

Christopher Wormell has asserted his right under
the Copyright, Designs and Patents Act, 1988, to
be identified as the author of this work

First published in the United Kingdom in 2001 by
Jonathan Cape, The Random House Group Limited
20 Vauxhall Bridge Road
London SW1V 2SA

The Random House Group Limited Reg. No. 954009
www.randomhouse.co.uk

A CIP catalogue record for this book is available
from the British Library

ISBN 0 224 04649 7

Printed in Hong Kong by Midas Printing Hong Kong